This little book about **Austin** belongs to:

_____

ISBN 978-0-9886347-0-1

Written by Allison Amador
Illustrated by Tammy Stanley
Published by Bee Cave Enterprises, LLC
Produced by Roger A. Amador, Jr.

This book was written, illustrated & printed in Austin, Texas.
Special thanks to Teri McCarthy and McCarthy Print.

For more information about the book visit us at:
www.goodnightaustintexas.com

Goodnight
AUSTIN™

A bedtime book for all who {heart} Austin

This book is dedicated to our beloved city - Austin, Texas & to our girls
Eavan, Elena & Ella
who are learning what makes **Austin** such an **amazing** place to live.

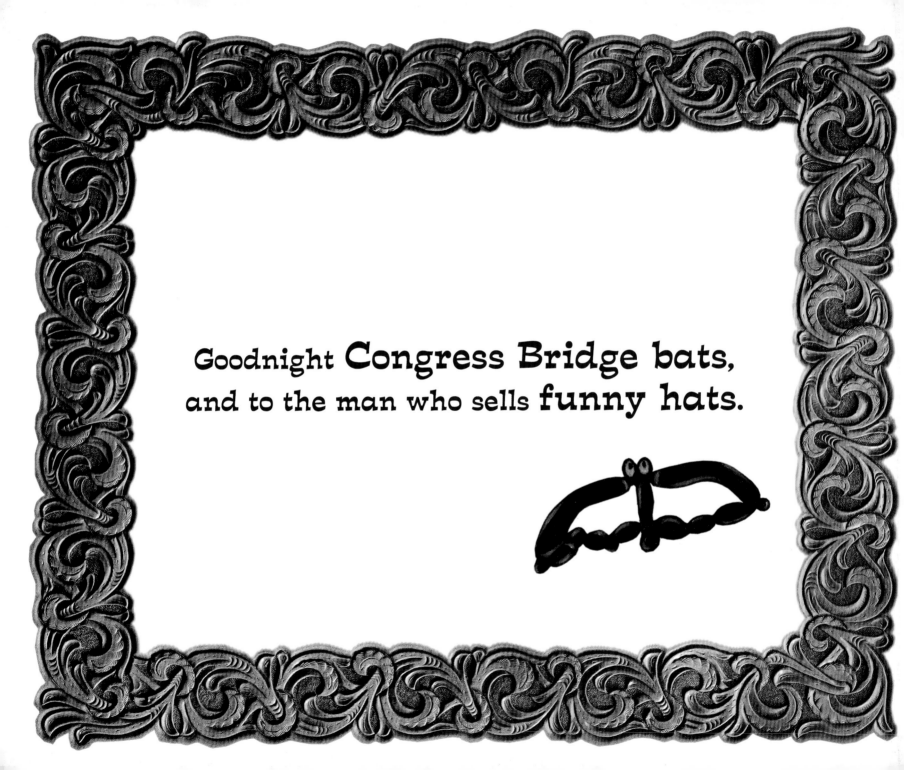

Goodnight **Congress Bridge bats,**
and to the man who sells **funny hats.**

Goodnight **Treaty Oak** with your branches so old,
Goodnight **hike & bike trail**, where we love to stroll.

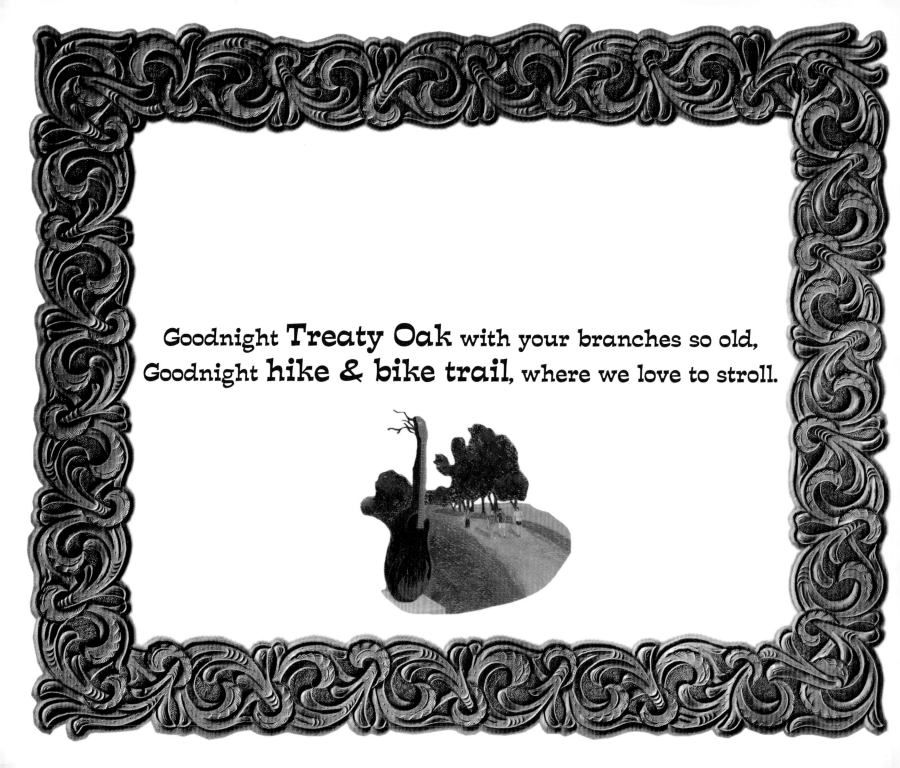

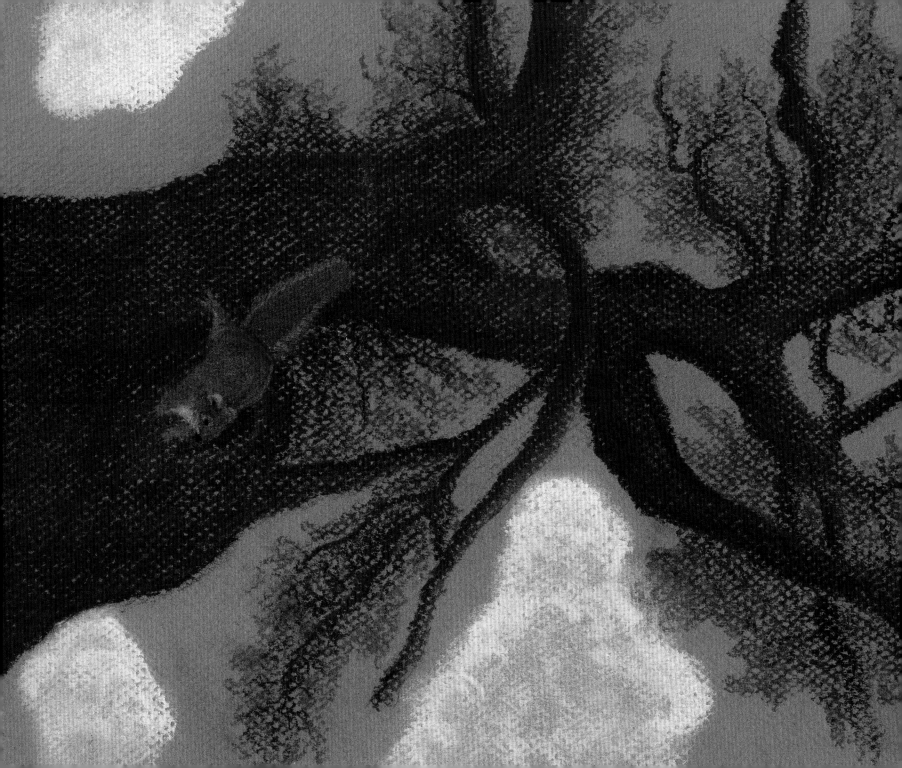

Goodnight cupcakes, Goodnight trailers.
Goodnight mariachis, Goodnight gospel players.

Goodnight **Amy's ice cream** on hot summer days,
Goodnight **wildflowers** that set highways ablaze.

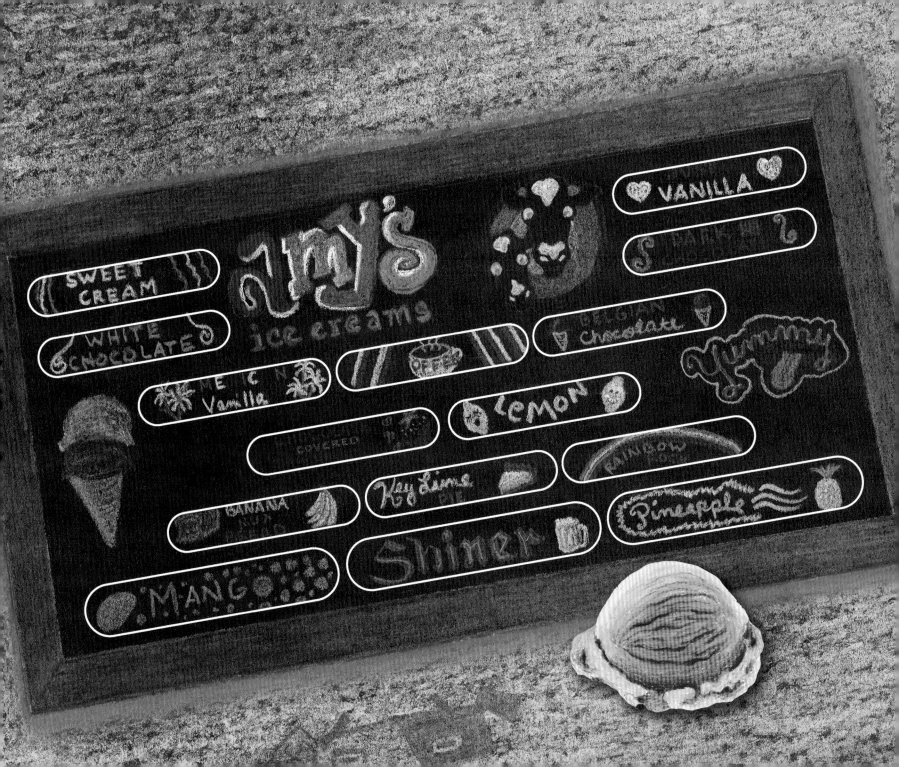

Goodnight **Barton Springs**, a gem to us all.
Goodnight **Peter Pan** looking so tall.

Goodnight **museum** with the great Texas star,
Goodnight **Stevie Ray** with your thrilling guitar.

Goodnight **Zilker train**, through the tunnel we go,
Goodnight **Children's Museum**, where our minds can grow.

Goodnight **Lake Austin** with your waters so green.
Goodnight **Lake Travis** with your sailboats that gleam.

Goodnight Longhorns and your tower that will say...
"The eyes of Texas are upon you, all the livelong day"

™

Goodnight to the kites over **Zilker Park**.
Goodnight Christmas lights, so dizzy after dark.

Goodnight to the animals at the Austin Zoo,
we're so happy they rescued you!

Goodnight cyclists crossing the **360 bridge**,
Goodnight **Nature Center** and the dino bones we dig.

Goodnight **Capitol** with your towering dome,
Goodnight to the trees the grackles call home.

Goodnight **Wildflower Center**, something's always in bloom,
I see your winding paths when dreaming in my room.

Goodnight **farmers' markets** and WHOLE FOODS MARKET

Your tasty treats put us in happy moods!

Goodnight **moonlight towers**, and thanks for your light, when I'm scared of the dark, you make things bright.

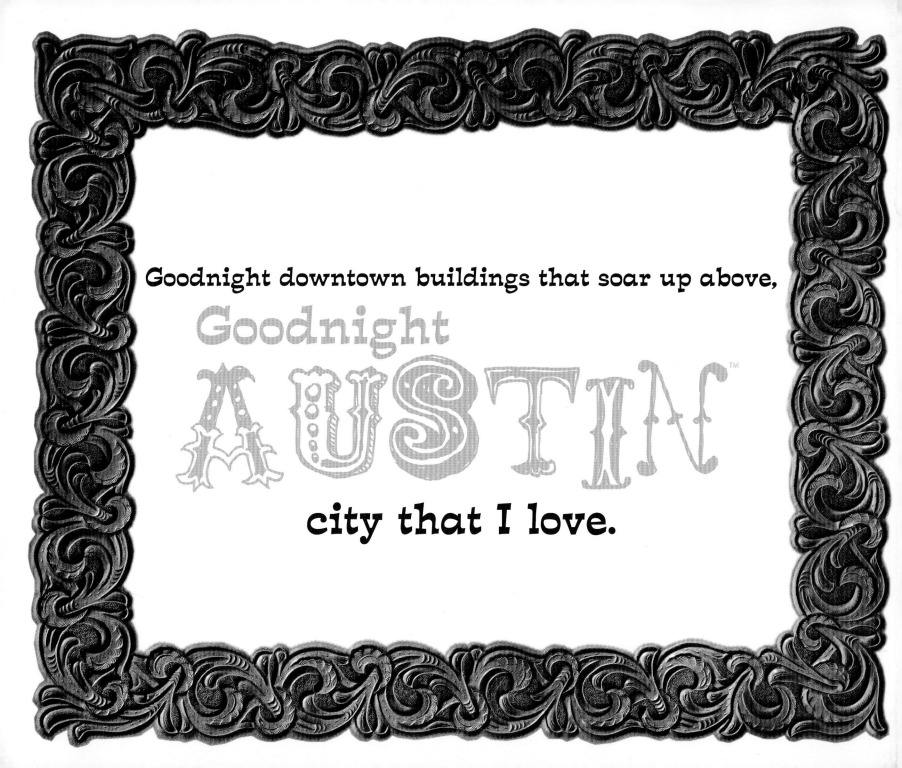

Goodnight downtown buildings that soar up above,

Goodnight AUSTIN™

city that I love.

In the summer, the world's largest urban bat colony of nearly 1.5 million Mexican free-tail bats emerge at dusk from under the **Congress Avenue Bridge** to feast on nearly 20,000 pounds of insects per night. Bring a blanket and picnic to the Austin American-Statesman Bat Observation Center and enjoy this uniquely Austin spectacle.

Legend says that in the 1830's, Stephen F. Austin negotiated the first Texas boundary treaty with Native American tribes under the 500-year old southern live oak known as **Treaty Oak**. The historic tree is located on Baylor Street between 5th and 6th streets.

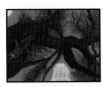

The scenic **Hike and Bike Trail** winds for ten miles along the water's edge of Lady Bird Lake, past skyscrapers, neighborhoods and some of Austin's most beautiful parks. This beloved trail represents the heart of Austin to many, where serious runners and casual strollers can enjoy Austin's outdoor culture.

The **Austin food trailer** scene began in earnest in 2009 when Hey Cupcake hoisted their eye-catching pink cupcake atop a shiny silver Air Stream trailer. Up-and-coming chefs quickly followed suit, offering creative dishes to hungry Austinites. Now, clusters of retro food trailers can be found on South Congress, South Lamar, South First Street, East 6th Street, and around the University of Texas campus.

Austin is considered the **Live Music Capital of the World**, boasting nearly 200 live music venues and playing host to the International SXSW Music Festival, the Austin City Limits Music Festival and many other outdoor musical events enjoyed by locals and visitors throughout the year.

With 13 locations throughout the city, **Amy's Ice Creams** has been winning the hearts and taste buds of Austinites since Amy Simmons opened her first location on Guadalupe Street in 1984. Indulging at Amy's is a uniquely Austin experience where staff entertain the customers and may give a free ice cream to anyone who will sing, dance or mimic a barnyard animal.

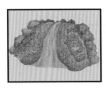

Every spring Texans eagerly await the explosion of color alongside highways when bluebonnets, Indian Paintbrushes and other **native wildflowers** take bloom. Photographing children in the midst of a bluebonnet patch is an annual rite of passage for many central Texas families.

Playing miniature golf in the shadow of the towering figure of its namesake, **Peter Pan Mini Golf** has been an Austin tradition since 1946. Head to Barton Springs Road to enjoy the quirky 18-hole courses that have kept their old-school feel intact.

Within Zilker Park's 358 acres lies one of Austin's crown jewels, **Barton Springs Pool**. This popular spring-fed swimming hole is over 900 feet long, and averages a refreshing 68 degrees, perfect for cooling off on hot summer days. The pool is also home to the endangered Barton Springs salamander that co-exists with year-round swimmers and visitors.

Head downtown to the 35-foot-tall bronze star sculpture in front of the **Bob Bullock Texas State History Museum,** where the history and legends that have shaped the Lone Star state come alive. With interactive exhibits, a special effects theater and IMAX theater, there is something to excite every age.

Visit the memorial statue of Austin guitar legend **Stevie Ray Vaughan** at Auditorium Shores near the First Street Bridge and enjoy one of the most iconic views of the downtown Austin skyline.

Delight the little ones with a 25-minute scenic ride on the **Zilker Zephyr Miniature Train** that traverses the shady shores of Lady Bird Lake and Barton Creek, and passes under a bridge where turtles, fish and swans may be spotted.

The **Thinkery**™ (The New Austin Children's Museum) is a fun, interactive, and creative learning center designed to inspire the next generation of problem solvers. Check out the exhibits and activities based in Science, Technology, Engineering, Art and Math (STEAM).

In and around Austin, are three reservoir lakes formed by the Colorado River. **Lady Bird Lake** is a beloved Austin centerpiece, and the green waters of **Lake Austin** wind through some of Austin's most beautiful landscapes. **Lake Travis** snakes 65 miles west of Mansfield Dam, and is a popular destination for boating, fishing, swimming, camping, picnicking and even scuba diving. Sailboats can always be seen reflecting the Texas sun on their sails.

A Texas longhorn steer named **Bevo** has been the University of Texas at Austin's mascot since 1916. The term "longhorns," refers to students and athletes alike and represents the pride and tradition of the university. "**The Eyes of Texas**," the alma mater of the University of Texas at Austin, was written by John Sinclair in 1903 and is set to the tune of "I've Been Working on the Railroad."

Thousands of kites sail over Zilker Park every spring at the **Zilker Kite Festival**, a staple in Austin family-friendly events. Established in 1929, it is the nation's oldest kite festival.

Spinning under the lights of the **Zilker Christmas Tree** with hot chocolate in hand is one of Austin's most popular holiday traditions. Standing 155-feet tall, the "tree" is composed of 3,300 multi-colored bulbs spiraling around a moonlight tower in Zilker park.

The **Austin Zoo and Animal Sanctuary,** with its rustic hill country feel, is a place where families can walk trails and catch a close-up view of more than 300 rescued animals.

The Pennybacker Bridge, better known as "**the 360 Bridge**," is an arched steel span across Lake Austin on scenic Highway 360. Whether driving or cycling across it, boating under it or hiking one of the cliffs above it, the 360 bridge is one of Austin's most scenic spots.

Located on the western edge of Zilker Park, the **Austin Nature and Science Center** invites children to explore the natural world with hands on exhibits, educational programs and recreation activities. Digging for fossils at the paleontology exhibit or "Dino Pit" is a kid favorite.

The **Texas Capitol,** sited on 22 acres of rolling lawns at one of Austin's highest points, anchors the downtown commercial district to the south and the University of Texas main campus just four blocks to the north. The distinctive red granite dome is 15 feet higher than the U.S. Capitol and can be seen from many vantage points throughout the city.

The **grackle,** a common black bird of North America, is so pervasive in the capitol city that Austinites consider it both a nuisance and a mascot of sorts.

The **Ladybird Johnson Wildflower Center** showcases the beauty and diversity of wildflowers and other native plants of central and southwest Texas. Public gardens, woodlands, meadows and educational programs teach families how to preserve this natural heritage and how to grow native plants in their own backyards.

Farmers' markets are held throughout the city every week to bring fresh produce, cheeses and meats directly from Central Texas farms. A visit to the Sunset Valley Farmers' Market on Saturdays is a treat for the kids with face painting, music and plenty of local treats.

Whole Foods Market first opened a small natural and organic foods store to the Austin community in 1980 and today has expanded to more than 310 stores worldwide. A visit to the flagship store on Lamar is an exciting shopping experience with food displays of every kind, a rooftop playground overlooking downtown and a winter holiday skating rink.

Austin is the only city in the world known to still operate **moonlight towers**, 165-foot tall, 15-foot wide lighting structures commonly used in the late 19th century to light city streets.

Goodnight Austin wishes to pay special tribute to local public artist **Dale Whistler**, whose sculpture "Night Wing" inspired the cover art for this book. The prominent bat-shaped sculpture, commemorating the largest urban bat colony in the U.S. may be seen swiveling in the breeze at the intersection of South Congress and Barton Springs Road. Whistlers sculptures, murals and signs can be seen throughout the city and are some of Austin's most recognizable and unique public artworks.